MAKING IT HOME

An Unofficial Minecraft® Adventure

JILL KEPPELER

An imprint of Enslow Publishing

WEST **44** BOOKS™

MINECRAFT® EXPLORERS

First Night
► **Making It Home** ◄
Staying Alive
Setting Forth

Please visit our website, www.west44books.com. For a free color catalog of all our high-quality books, call toll free 1-800-542-2595 or fax 1-877-542-2596.

Cataloging-in-Publication Data

Names: Keppeler, Jill.

Title: Making it home: an unofficial Minecraft adventure / Jill Keppeler.

Description: New York : West 44, 2020. | Series: Minecraft® explorers

Identifiers: ISBN 9781538384114 (pbk.) | ISBN 9781538384176 (library bound) | ISBN 9781538384060 (ebook)

Subjects: LCSH: Minecraft (Game)--Juvenile fiction. | Video games--Juvenile fiction. | Sisters--Juvenile fiction.

Classification: LCC PZ7.K477 Ma 2020 | DDC [F]--dc23

First Edition

Published in 2020 by
Enslow Publishing LLC
101 West 23rd Street, Suite #240
New York, NY 10011

Copyright © 2020 Enslow Publishing LLC

Editor: Caitie McAneney
Designer: Seth Hughes
Cover Designer: Haley Harasymiw

CPSIA compliance information: Batch #CS19W44: For further information contact
Enslow Publishing LLC, New York, New York at 1-800-542-2595.

To Jimmy
Keep doing your own thing!

MEET THE CHARACTERS

► MATT LOPEZ ◄

Matt's an ordinary kid. He loves his parents, squabbles with his sister and brother, does pretty well in school, and has a group of good friends with whom he plays *Minecraft*. But sometimes, even an ordinary kid likes to have an adventure—and when Matt acquires a virtual reality headset from a mysterious neighbor, he finds himself in the middle of something really remarkable: an actual *Minecraft* world!

► DAVE LEE ◄

Dave knows he's not as adventurous as his best friend, Matt. He's OK with that! He likes to know what he's getting into, and he likes to be prepared for it. But there are some things you can't really prepare for, and going into a real *Minecraft* world is one of them. If Dave has anything to say about it, though, their *Minecraft* base will be a lot more prepared when he's done with it.

► JASMINE "JAZ" JACKSON ◄

Jaz is creative and artistic. She loves making things, and she loves working with colors. She also likes being a twin, and she loves her twin sister, Kayla. But sometimes, people like to put them in little boxes, like "the creative one" versus "the adventurous one." When Jaz gets her chance to go into a real *Minecraft* world, she'll get the chance to show that she can be both, all on her own.

► KAYLA JACKSON ◄

Kayla's usually the first to jump into adventures with her sister and her friends. Still, even she's a little cautious about leaping into an actual *Minecraft* world! Once there, though, Kayla's curiosity and fondness for exploring might lead her into trouble—but also into learning a lot more about the world she and her friends have found. And by the time she's done, they might have some new opportunities for adventure.

CHAPTER ONE
IT'S
UNBELIEVABLE
. . . .

Jasmine Jackson liked to think she had a pretty open mind.

She had a good imagination. She always listened and took part when her friends told ghost stories. She loved the folktales her Grandma Ibori told her. And her teachers always told her how creative her artwork was.

But this? This might be a bit too much.

"Not funny, Matt," Jasmine's twin sister, Kayla, said in an annoyed voice. She was talking to their friend Matt Lopez. "You're right. I don't believe you."

The four of them—Jaz and Kayla, Matt and their friend Dave Lee—were sitting in Matt's backyard. Matt had sent them a message late the night before. He said he had something important to tell them. And he said they wouldn't believe it.

He was right!

They all went to Matt's house after school. Matt had dragged them all out back so his little brother wouldn't bother them. Then, he'd told them that he'd bought a virtual reality headset the day before, at a lawn sale. The sale had been at the big black house they called the EnderHouse.

And when he'd put the headset on, he said, he'd been transported into a *Minecraft* world!

"I believe him," Dave said. He was sitting carefully on a chair he'd dragged over from the patio. The rest of them were sitting on Matt's old swing set. But Dave had fallen off one of the swings last year. Now he refused to use it. He said it was bad luck.

Kayla made a slightly rude noise as she spun around, twisting the chains of her swing together. Annoyed, Jaz reached out and shoved at her sister's leg with one foot. That just made Kayla laugh.

"No, really," Dave insisted. "He couldn't make up something this weird." He leaned back against the chair. "And he wouldn't try to trick us with it if he did."

"Yeah!" Matt said, defending himself. He was sitting at the top of the slide. His legs were stretched out on the slope. "I wouldn't. You guys know me better than that."

"Remember last April Fools' Day?" Kayla asked him. But Matt shook his head.

"That was just a prank," he said. Jaz remembered the cookies stuffed with toothpaste that he'd brought to school on

April 1. Ew! "And it's not even April."

"Maybe you dreamed it?" Jaz asked, speaking up. "You said when you took the helmet off, it was morning."

Matt bit his lip. He looked uncertain. "Yeah. But this was really … real. And it hurt when the skeleton shot me." He put a hand on his shoulder. "The water was cold. And I was really hungry when I was healing. I could *feel* all those things."

"You can be cold in dreams," Kayla pointed out, spinning on her swing in the other direction. "I dreamed I was stuck out in the snow once. I was freezing!" She giggled, putting her feet down to stop. "When I woke up, Jaz had stolen my blanket."

Jaz rolled her eyes, but she kept thinking.

"There's one way to test it, Matt," she said, slowly. "Could someone else try it? And see what happens?"

FACT: SKELETONS IN *MINECRAFT* SHOOT ARROWS AT YOU. SOMETIMES, A SKELETON MIGHT MISS YOU AND HIT ANOTHER SKELETON. THEN THE SKELETONS WILL FIRE AT EACH OTHER!

"Not me," Dave said immediately. But Matt nodded.

"It's OK with me," he said. "But who?"

Kayla looked uncertain. That was a little unusual. She was usually eager to try new things. She didn't look eager right now.

People always tended to put the twins in categories. They didn't always like that. Jaz was often called "the creative one" or "the artistic one." Kayla was "the brave one" or "the athletic one."

Well, Jaz could be the brave one, too.

"I'll do it," she said, standing up as the others stared at her. "Tonight."

CHAPTER TWO

SISTER'S KEEPER

. . . .

Jaz didn't have to carry the VR headset far. The sisters only lived down at the end of the street.

That was how they'd met Matt and Dave. There had been a big block party only a few days after they'd moved in. The girls had attended with their parents.

Mr. and Dr. Jackson started talking to other grown-ups. But Jaz and Kayla had noticed two boys sitting on one house's porch. The boys were peering at their tablets.

Kayla heard the word "creeper." She bounded up onto the porch before Jaz could stop her.

"Hey," she'd called. "Are you playing *Minecraft*? Can we play too?"

The boys could have been jerks. But instead, Matt and Dave had welcomed Jaz and Kayla to their *Minecraft* realm.

Later, Matt's parents had chased them off the porch and down to the party. That had been fun, too.

"Have a good day at school, girls?" Dad was in the kitchen when Jaz emerged from the bedroom. He was washing his hands. Kayla was already sitting at the table, eating carrot sticks. She made a face at Jaz. Jaz made a face back.

Dad said he was a carpenter. But Mom said he was an artist. Jaz thought he was both. He made beautiful things out of wood in his workshop in their garage.

Dad made furniture and carvings and sometimes toys. Jaz loved to watch him work with all the kinds of wood. He used oak and birch, spruce and maple and ash. They all looked different!

That was one of the reasons Jaz liked to build things in *Minecraft*. There were only six kinds of wood in the game, but they all looked different. Just like the woods her dad worked with!

 FACT: *MINECRAFT* OAK WOOD IS A MEDIUM BROWN. DARK OAK IS VERY DARK BROWN. SPRUCE WOOD IS SOMEWHERE BETWEEN THE TWO. BIRCH WOOD IS PALE. ACACIA WOOD IS AN ORANGE COLOR; AND JUNGLE WOOD IS TAN.

"Mom made mac and cheese earlier and put it in the fridge," Dad said, smiling. Both girls grinned at each other. Homemade macaroni and cheese was a treat! "It's in the oven now. Broccoli or green beans with it?"

"Broccoli," Jaz said. Kayla said, "Green beans!" They made faces at each other again.

Dad broke the tie and picked green beans. Jaz shrugged. She pulled her math book out of her backpack. She wanted to start her homework now. If she did, she might be able to watch TV with Dad later.

Their mom was a doctor who worked at the local hospital. Dr. Janelle Jackson had a long overnight shift tonight. The girls would see her when they got home from school tomorrow.

Dinner was delicious. (Even the green beans.) After their homework was done, Dad said they could watch TV. The three of them watched silly TV shows for a while. Then Dad told them it was time for bed.

Jaz hugged him goodnight and nearly ran to their room. Kayla followed more slowly.

The girls got ready for bed. Then Jaz

picked up the headset. She plugged it into their game system. Then she started *Minecraft*.

Kayla sat cross-legged on her desk chair, watching her.

"Are you really sure you want to do this?" she asked.

"Yes!" Jaz ran a hand over her head, smoothing her braids. They should be fine with the headset, she decided. The beads at the end of each braid wouldn't get in the way.

"Don't you think it might be … dangerous?"

Jaz blinked and looked up at her sister.

"Kay," she asked, surprised. "Are you *worried*?" Kayla never worried! At least, she never seemed to.

Her sister glanced away. "A little," she admitted. Then she looked back at Jaz. "This is just weird."

Jaz grinned at her. "I know!" she said.

"That's why I like it." She carefully put the headset on. Then she settled down on the bottom bunk.

"Don't take off the headset off," she told Kayla. "Not until morning."

Kayla sighed. "OK," she said. "But I'm watching you for a while. Just to make sure you're all right."

Jaz smiled. Her sister really did care. "Thank you."

Then she tapped the button on the headset once, like Matt told her. Then she did it again. Then she did it a third time.

There was a bright flash of purple! Jaz closed her eyes.

CHAPTER THREE

THE CAVE SHELTER

· · · ·

There were purple sparkles in front of Jaz's eyes. She blinked again. Her vision started to clear.

She was staring up at a gray stone ceiling. This really wasn't home!

Carefully, Jaz sat up. She looked around. She was in a small room. Or a small cave? The walls were gray stone, too.

Everything was blocky and made of cubes. In one corner, there was a cube of wood. It had a grid on top and markings that looked like tools. A crafting table! Jaz was definitely in *Minecraft*.

She stood up and turned around. There
was a cube of stone with different markings. A
furnace! There was also a little wooden chest.
There were a few torches on the walls.

 FACT: YOU CAN
MAKE A CHEST IN
MINECRAFT OUT
OF EIGHT WOODEN
PLANKS. EACH
CHEST HAS 27 SLOTS
TO HOLD ITEMS.
TWO CHESTS SIDE
BY SIDE MAKE A
DOUBLE CHEST THAT
HOLDS 54 ITEMS.

At one end of the little room, there
were glass windows and a door. Jaz could see
daylight outside. She smiled. Yes! This was
so cool!

She looked down. Like Matt had said, she
didn't look like a blocky *Minecraft* avatar. She
was wearing jeans and a purple T-shirt instead

of her purple pajamas.

Jaz held her hands up in front of her face. Her smile grew. Her skin was its familiar deep brown color. Usually, if she wanted that in *Minecraft*, she needed to make or buy a special avatar.

She shook her head and heard the beads on her braids rattle together quietly. Her hair was the same, too. Excellent.

Jaz moved over to the small chest and opened it. It was a little odd. She could see the items in the chest floating in a grid. Some were much smaller than they'd be usually. Otherwise, how could someone fit up to 64 blocks of cobblestone in a one slot? But that was how *Minecraft* worked.

Jaz reached out and touched the shape of a bright red apple. Immediately, it moved toward her and vanished. But if she closed her eyes, she could still see it. In fact, there were three apples there.

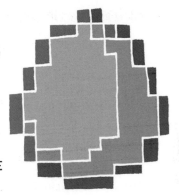

FACT: IN PERSONAL INVENTORIES AND CHESTS IN *MINECRAFT*, MANY ITEMS WILL STACK UP TO 64 IN ONE SLOT. SOME ITEMS (INCLUDING EGGS) WILL STACK UP TO 16. SOME ITEMS (SUCH AS WEAPONS) CAN ONLY BE STORED ONE PER SLOT.

Matt had explained how inventories worked here. She could carry things with her this way.

Jaz studied the other items in her mind's eye. She must have the same inventory that Matt carried when he went to sleep here. She also had some blocks of oak wood and oak planks. She had a shiny iron sword and a battered stone pickaxe. Those were all useful things.

In the chest, there were a few pieces of coal, some torches, and a pair of shears. There was a wooden axe and a wooden shovel. There were a few other items, too, such as many blocks of cobblestone.

Jaz didn't want to carry that all with her. She decided to keep the things she already had. She also took the coal, torches, shears, and axe. That was enough for now.

Then she walked over to the door, opened it, and stepped into a real, live *Minecraft* landscape.

"I can't believe this," she whispered, closing the door behind her. "This is great."

Jaz took a few steps. She could hear the sound of the grass and then sand crunching under her feet.

The sky was blue above her, with blocky white clouds. The sound of the water at her feet was just like that of running water at home. The sunshine from the square yellow sun was warm on her face. Jaz smiled.

Then she heard the "hisssssss … " from her left.

CHAPTER FOUR

I HATE CREEPERS

. . . .

Boom!

Jaz gasped, struggling up on her elbows in the cold water of the stream. She'd thrown herself to the side when she'd heard the creeper's hiss.

It took a minute for her to realize that she was unhurt. She'd moved just far enough away. The creeper explosion hadn't affected her.

She couldn't say the same for the cave shelter, though. The door was gone. The windows were gone. Almost all the cobblestone on the front was gone.

And there was a big pit right where the

door had been. Tiny versions of the door, a few torches, and some cobblestone, sand, and dirt blocks floated there.

But the stone had shielded the shelter a little. The crafting table, chest, furnace, and bed were still whole inside.

Jaz took a deep breath. She was shaking. This world suddenly seemed a lot scarier!

"I hate creepers," she said to herself. She climbed to her feet. The water ran right off her, leaving her dry. "I *really* hate creepers."

Would Matt be upset when he heard about the shelter? No, she decided, stepping closer to the wreckage. Matt understood about creepers. They were a real pain in *Minecraft*!

Some of the water from the stream was flowing into the pit. *Minecraft* water didn't work like real-world water. The pit wouldn't fill up. Still, Jaz picked up a few blocks of dirt. She used it to rebuild a bit of the shore. That blocked the water.

Then she carefully moved down into the pit.

 FACT: CREEPERS ARE GREEN *MINECRAFT* CREATURES WITH ARMLESS BODIES AND FOUR SHORT LEGS. THEY CAN GO OUT IN DAYLIGHT WHEN MANY MOBS CAN'T. THEY'RE SILENT AND SNEAKY— AT LEAST UNTIL THEY BLOW UP!

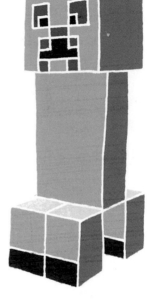

It was weird and a little scary. She could jump down two blocks at a time. That was about her height!

Jaz made it to the bottom. Then she climbed up the other side. She could jump about a block at a time. Whoosh! That was kind of fun.

The exposed shelter looked sort of sad. Jaz stood there and looked around. She felt a little sad, too. It had taken Matt a lot of work to make this. And, boom, it was gone in seconds.

Still, Matt had admitted it was just a survival shelter. It was just a place to spend his first night in *Minecraft*. It was a way to shut out the monsters. Once a player collected enough resources, he or she could build something better.

Jaz smiled. She knew what she'd do! She'd make a new shelter. Better yet: a small house! A house could have more windows. That way, she could see creepers or other monsters before she stepped out the door. And they could all share it when they visited this world.

Walking over to the chest, Jaz took out the other supplies. Then she chopped down the crafting table. She picked up the tiny version of it. She mined the furnace. She picked that up, too.

Jaz picked up all the pieces of dirt that the explosion had created. She filled in the creeper pit as much as she could. She grumbled about creepers the whole time!

Then, she used the cobblestone that had

been in the chest. She quickly walled off the front of the shelter. That way, she could use the space again if she needed it. She made sure there were enough torches inside. She put one of the extra doors in front.

FACT: *MINECRAFT* MONSTERS SPAWN IN THE DARK. MAKE SURE YOU HAVE PLENTY OF TORCHES FOR A SHELTER! ONE STICK AND ONE PIECE OF COAL OR CHARCOAL MAKE FOUR TORCHES.

Then Jaz took another deep breath. She looked up at the sun. Then she reached into her inventory and pulled out her iron sword.

"Here we go," she said to herself. "Time to explore."

CHAPTER FIVE

GONE FISHING

. . . .

Matt had given Jaz a basic idea of the area
around the shelter. She climbed the hill
(climbing was fun!) and looked for the trees. It
was always a good idea to have plenty of pieces
of wood in *Minecraft*. And she could use wood
planks in the house.

She saw the little forest in the distance.
She'd have to cross the plain. Jaz looked
around, but she didn't see any monsters. There
were some black-and-white moving shapes.
Cows? Cows couldn't hurt her. She gripped her
iron sword and started walking.

The plain was flat and green. Jaz looked around as she walked. There were some scattered flowers and tufts of grass. Plains were one of the most boring *Minecraft* biomes. But right now, she was glad for something boring! She made it across the plain without a problem. Then she stared up at the nearest oak tree.

FACT: DIFFERENT *MINECRAFT* TOOLS WORK FASTER ON DIFFERENT MATERIALS. TO CHOP WOOD, AN AXE WORKS BEST. SHOVELS WORK BEST ON DIRT, SAND, AND GRAVEL, AND PICKAXES WORK BEST ON STONE.

"OK," she said to herself, closing her eyes. "I need an axe."

The wooden axe in her inventory was chipped, but it would work for now. Jaz pulled it out and swung it at the tree. Chop! Chop! Chop! She turned the tree trunk into chunks of wood. Then she collected them and went to another tree. Chop!

"Moo," one of the cows commented as she collected the wood.

Jaz laughed at it. "Moo?" she told the cow. "What does that mean? Does it mean, 'Good job, Jasmine?'"

"Moo!"

That's when Jaz heard it: the skittering sound of a spider.

Spiders in *Minecraft* wouldn't attack you in the daylight. Not unless you attacked them first! But Jaz knew that if she killed a spider, it might drop string. With string, she could make a bow or a fishing pole.

Jaz snatched her iron sword out of her inventory. She spun around. There! In the trees! The shiny red eyes of a spider. It was creeping around, doing whatever *Minecraft* spiders did during the day. (Which didn't seem to be much.)

Spiders could climb things. Then they could jump down and attack you. A forest was not a good place to fight a spider. Jaz needed a plan.

She thought a minute. Then, she ran forward and swung her sword at the spider. Hiss! It connected. The spider was knocked back a little. Jaz turned and ran!

Skitter, skitter! She could hear the spider behind her. But as soon as she was out onto the plain again, Jaz turned. She swung the sword again. Hiss! The spider couldn't climb anything and jump down at her. It lunged again. But Jaz swung again. The blow connected.

Poof, the spider was gone! It left behind two little bits of floating string. Jaz grabbed them and waved them in the air.

"Whoooo!" she yelled. "Take that!

"Moo," commented the cow.

"Yeah, thanks for the tip," Jaz told it, grinning. She pulled out her crafting table and placed it on the ground, then used the string and three sticks to make a fishing rod.

This was a great tool to have, she knew. If you had a fishing pole and a pool or stream of water in *Minecraft*, you could always get food. And she wanted more food in her inventory before she went to find a cave to get some more building materials.

Picking up her crafting table, she hurried back across the plain and down the hill to the stream. There, she cast the bobber end of the fishing pole into the water and waited.

And waited.

Jaz yawned and looked overhead. The sun was nearly right above her now. She had to get moving if she was going to get anything done. Right then, however, she saw a sparkle in the water out of the corner of her eye. She looked back down at her fishing pole. Sploosh! Something pulled the bobber underwater.

Jaz yanked at the pole. A small reddish shape flew out of the water. She caught it. A salmon!

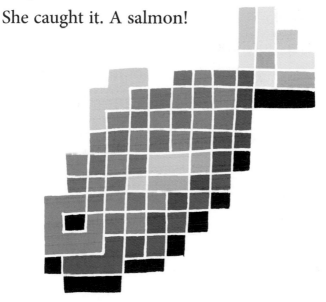

FACT: THERE ARE FOUR KINDS OF FISH IN *MINECRAFT*: SALMON, COD (SOMETIMES JUST CALLED "FISH"), TROPICAL FISH, AND PUFFERFISH. A PLAYER CAN EAT SALMON AND COD. PUFFERFISH ARE POISONOUS, BUT THEY CAN BE USED IN POTIONS.

Perfect.

Just like that, the fish started biting. Jaz set up her furnace and cooked the salmon and whitish cod as she caught them. Of course, fish weren't all a fishing pole could catch in *Minecraft*. Sometimes you could catch junk or treasure, too. She also pulled in two more strings, a lily pad, and a pair of leather boots. She pulled the boots onto her feet. They weren't in good shape. But they'd do until she made better armor.

Yes, a fishing pole was a good tool to have.

CHAPTER SIX
DEEPER DOWN
. . . .

Matt had also told Jaz about the cave where he'd found coal and iron—and a skeleton. He had told her about his mysterious rescuer, too. At the time, Jaz wasn't sure she believed him about that. This whole thing sounded weird enough without mystery characters.

Now, she wasn't sure.

Jaz started to the right, along the river. The sand and the gravel of the shore crunched under her feet. Soon, she saw the cave Matt had mentioned. Taking a deep breath, she crossed the river, moving through the chilly water. She was glad how quickly she dried off in this *Minecraft* world!

Matt had gone into the cave without torches. Jaz wasn't going to do that. She placed one right at the entrance. Then, as she moved into the cave, she placed them every eight blocks or so. That way, monsters wouldn't spawn. She could also see better to find resources.

Jaz knew that it was a good idea to put torches along only on one side of a cave wall. That way, if she got lost, she could find her way out. But this cave didn't seem that big. She just put the torches down wherever. There were too many other things to focus on.

She collected two stacks of gray cobblestone pretty quickly. Then she collected some granite, diorite, and andesite. She might want variety in the house! And there were a few good seams of coal. The cave sloped, block by block, deeper into the ground.

NOTE: DIORITE IS A SPECKLED WHITE ROCK BLOCK IN *MINECRAFT*. GRANITE IS A SPECKLED PINKISH ROCK, AND ANDESITE IS A SILVER-GRAY BLOCK. IN THE REAL WORLD, ALL THREE TYPES OF ROCK ARE IGNEOUS. THAT MEANS THEY'RE FORMED BY MAGMA, HOT LIQUID ROCK INSIDE EARTH.

Then Jaz reached a place where the cave split. Part went off to the right, while part sloped farther downward to the left. Jaz put a torch right at the split. She looked around.

Was that … ? Yes! Jaz hurried for the left side, jumping down block by block. Iron ore! A lot of iron ore!

Jaz swung her old stone pickaxe at the iron

ore. She only managed to carve out three pieces when it broke. But that was OK. Setting up her furnace, she smelted the ore. Then she used the three iron ingots to make an iron pickaxe.

She finished collecting all the iron ore in the cave wall. Then she looked around again. The cave continued downward. She had plenty of torches and a new pickaxe. She had her iron sword in case she ran into monsters. Exploring was fun!

So Jaz kept mining. She chose her path based on where she saw resources. She turned at intersection after intersection. Often, she doubled back. She ate some salmon and an apple. She collected stacks of coal and more iron ore. She put torches wherever to light things up.

She thought about the tough iron armor she'd make. She killed a stray zombie with her sword. Then she killed a spider, getting two more pieces of string.

FACT: DIAMOND IS THE TOUGHEST MATERIAL IN *MINECRAFT* FOR TOOLS AND ARMOR. BUT IRON IS FAR MORE COMMON. YOU CAN ALSO MAKE MANY OTHER ITEMS, SUCH AS ANVILS, SHEARS, AND BUCKETS, OUT OF IRON.

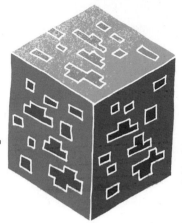

After a little while, she knew she was deep beneath the surface. The cave system was still and quiet. It was dark as the cave went even deeper. Jaz knew it was probably time to go back up. She was almost out of wood with which to make torches and new tools.

She looked regretfully toward the darkness. Who knew what cool resources were in there? Then she turned back.

Jaz did just fine until she got to the first big cave intersection. Then she paused. She'd thought she'd remember which path. But it wasn't that easy. Paths went off in about six different directions. And that was just from this hub!

She picked a route, but it quickly led her to a dead end. Another choice led her to another intersection, then another. But soon her choices led her to another dark cave. She hadn't been this way before.

Jaz circled back. She was starting to get alarmed. She went down one path, then another. She took a tumble into a pit. She ate some more salmon. A skeleton attack (Matt was right! Those arrows stung!) meant that she had to eat even more to heal.

Then she emerged into another intersection. Or was it? Jaz noticed a pyramid of granite blocks. She realized she was back in the first intersection. She'd gone in a circle.

Jaz wanted to sit down and cry. She was hopelessly lost!

CHAPTER SEVEN
LOST!
. . . .

Jaz sat down on a block of stone and stared at the cave around her. Passages went off in all directions. She had no idea where to go.

It was such a noob mistake to get lost in a cave system! Jaz knew how to mark her way. But she just hadn't bothered. She'd been sure she'd just know. It'd been so exciting to explore!

She tried to stay calm and think about her choices. Her mom told her to make lists of choices and their pros and cons when she had a decision to make. It worked! But there didn't seem to be any good decisions here.

She could just start walking, trying tunnel after tunnel. But the hours of daylight were running out. She could try digging upward. There were many problems with that idea, though.

 FACT: ONE BIG RULE OF *MINECRAFT* IS NEVER TO DIG STRAIGHT UP OR STRAIGHT DOWN. IF YOU DIG STRAIGHT UP, YOU COULD SUFFOCATE IF GRAVEL OR SAND FALL ON YOU. YOU COULD DROWN IF YOU HIT WATER. OR YOU COULD HIT A PATCH OF LAVA!

Jaz looked down at the pickaxe in her hand. It was starting to wear out. She'd have to smelt more iron for a new one. Or, she could make a more fragile stone one. But the bigger problem was that she didn't have much wood left. She checked her inventory. She just had a few wooden planks. She should have paid more attention to that, too.

Jaz looked around again.

Then she saw the figure.

It was just a flash of green at first. That's what caught her eye. The last thing she needed was a creeper! But the figure didn't move like a creeper—or moan like a zombie. It was at the mouth of a passageway leading to the left. Jaz stood up. She thought she heard the crunch of footsteps on dirt.

"Hi?" she called. "Is someone there?"

The figure turned away and Jaz blinked. She thought she saw a flash of something reddish-orange.

"Wait!" she called, moving forward. Maybe this mysterious figure knew the way back to the surface!

The figure didn't wait. Jaz started to run.

She leapt up a few blocks and into the

passageway. She'd been here already and the area was well lit. Looking around, she saw a bit of green again and followed.

FACT: THERE ARE FIVE DIFFERENT KINDS OF ZOMBIES IN *MINECRAFT*: REGULAR ZOMBIES, ZOMBIE VILLAGERS, HUSKS, ZOMBIE PIGMEN, AND DROWNED. EACH TYPE HAS A BABY ZOMBIE VERSION, TOO.

For the next few minutes, all Jaz heard were the crunch of footsteps on stone and dirt and the sound of her own breathing. The figure didn't make another sound. But it continued to stay just within sight, barely. It made one turn after another. Jaz followed.

Finally, Jaz skidded to halt. She realized she could see daylight up ahead. And there was a figure in the cave opening.

It was a familiar blocky *Minecraft* shape, wearing brown pants and a light green shirt. Reddish-orange hair hung in a single braid over one shoulder. The figure had green eyes and pale skin, like Dave's.

"Thank you!" Jaz called breathlessly. "Thank you!"

The figure nodded.

And then it was gone.

CHAPTER EIGHT

FOUNDATION, WALLS, AND ROOF

. . . .

Jaz was surprised as she stepped out of the cave. Not as much time had passed as she'd feared! It was still midday. She breathed a huge sigh of relief. It was time to get building.

She hurried back toward the shelter and climbed the hill. She'd already decided to build the house there, on the plain. There would be a lot of room to expand later if they wanted. And it was always good to build your base close to your spawn point.

First, Jaz studied the area. She came up

with a plan. She decided to put the front door facing the river. It would be a nice view.

FACT: YOU CAN MAKE A COMPASS IN *MINECRAFT* OUT OF FOUR IRON INGOTS AND A PIECE OF REDSTONE DUST. A COMPASS WILL ALWAYS POINT BACK TO YOUR SPAWN POINT. IF YOU BUILD YOUR BASE NEAR THIS SPOT, YOU CAN ALWAYS USE A COMPASS TO FIND YOUR WAY HOME.

Then she took out her shovel. She started to dig out some dirt, just one block down. She dug a rectangle, eight blocks by six blocks. Then she put blocks of cobblestone in that rectangle. That would be the house's foundation.

Jaz planned to use cobblestone for the whole house right now. It didn't look as nice as wood or stone or clay bricks. But it was tough and easy to find. She figured they could always spruce it up later.

It was sure a lot easier to build a *Minecraft* house than a real one! The stone cubes were half her size. But she could lift and place them easily.

"Oink?"

Jaz looked up from admiring her work. A pink pig was standing there, watching her.

"Hello!" she told it. "It's nice to have some company."

"Oink."

"Just stay out of the way, or I'll have to turn you into pork chops."

"*Oink.*"

Next, Jaz placed more cobblestone blocks around the edge of the foundation. Those would be the walls of the house. She used them to build a doorframe. Then she placed the oak door from the shelter in the frame.

"Oops!" she told the pig, which was shuffling about, thinking piggy thoughts. "I forgot about windows."

The pig didn't comment.

Jaz started some sand smelting into glass in a furnace nearby. Then she continued to build walls. She left spaces for windows in the walls as she built them up.

The house would be very gray, she thought. They were going to need some color. But first, they just needed walls and a roof.

For the roof, Jaz used some cobblestone to make cobblestone stairs. Stairs could be used to make a peaked roof. Jaz thought it looked a little better than a flat one.

Then she took the glass blocks out of the furnace. She used her crafting table to turn them into panes. Then she filled in the window frames.

 FACT: ONE SMELTED BLOCK OF SAND MAKES ONE GLASS BLOCK. YOU CAN USE SIX GLASS BLOCKS TO MAKE 16 GLASS PANES, WHICH ARE FLAT SHEETS OF GLASS. YOU ALSO CAN USE DYE ON THEM TO MAKE STAINED GLASS.

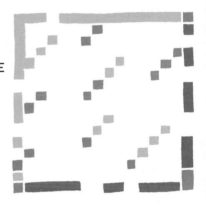

And just like that, she had a house.

Jaz stepped back outside. Then she turned to look at the little stone house. She put her hands on her hips and smiled.

It was very small. It was very plain. But they could store their stuff in it. And it would keep out the monsters. It was home!

CHAPTER NINE

ADDING SOME COLOR

· · · ·

The new house was done, but it was bare! Jaz placed her crafting table and furnace inside. She put the 32 pieces of iron ore she'd collected in the cave system into the furnace to smelt. She added four pieces of coal as fuel.

Then she went back to the old shelter and collected the bed and the chest. She'd keep the shelter intact, just in case. But the bed should definitely stay in the house. When you slept on a *Minecraft* bed, it reset your spawn point.

But as she climbed the hill back to the

house, she thought about how plain and gray it was. Even the bed was just plain white. It really needed some color. And she'd seen flowers (and a few sheep) out on the plain.

Jaz looked up at the sun. It was getting really low in the sky. Soon, the sky would start to get pink as the sun set. But she had a little time.

The *Minecraft* sheep ignored her as she sheared them, collecting four cubes of white wool. Then she hurried toward the scattering of flowers.

FACT: THERE ARE 15 KINDS OF FLOWERS IN *MINECRAFT*. TEN OF THESE KINDS ARE ONE BLOCK HIGH AND FIVE OF THESE KINDS ARE TWO BLOCKS HIGH. NOT ALL FLOWERS GROW IN EVERY BIOME.

The yellow ones were dandelions. Sometimes Jaz picked dandelions from her yard at home. She collected a handful of them. Then she looked for the red flowers she'd seen. Those were poppies. She'd never seen real poppies before, but they were common on *Minecraft* plains. She collected some of those, too.

Crunch! The sheep behind her had lowered its head to the grass. A patch of green disappeared, leaving plain dirt behind. The sheep's wool regrew instantly. Jaz grinned and sheared it again. Now she had seven cubes of wool. She waited a moment and the other sheep ate some grass too. Snip! Now she had eight cubes.

The sun was starting to set when Jaz got back to the house. She closed the door, smiling, pleased she had such a sturdy home. Then she walked over to the crafting table.

You could make red dye out of poppies, red tulips, rosebushes, or beetroots. Jaz turned her five poppies into five pieces of red dye. Then she made yellow dye out of the dandelions.

Jaz had learned about combining colors in art class. Purple was her favorite color. She'd like to make some purple dye, but she'd need blue to combine with the red for that. In *Minecraft*, you could only make blue out of lapis lazuli, a stone. She hadn't found any lapis lazuli ore in the cave.

 FACT: LAPIS LAZULI ORE IS ONLY FOUND DEEP UNDERGROUND IN *MINECRAFT*. EACH PIECE OF ORE DROPS FOUR TO EIGHT PIECES OF LAPIS LAZULI. LAPIS LAZULI IS A REAL-WORLD GEMSTONE.

Jaz thought a minute. Then she put a piece of red dye on the crafting table with a piece of yellow dye.

Now she had two pieces of orange dye! Jaz liked orange, too. She used the dye on the white bed. Then she placed the orange bed down in a corner of the room. The bright color looked even brighter in the gray house.

Jaz looked down at the stone floor. Then she smiled. She used two pieces of red dye on two blocks of white wool. Two pieces of red wool made three squares of red carpet! She put them on the floor.

Now the house was really starting to look more like a home.

CHAPTER 10
HOME TO HOME

. . . .

Jaz stood at one of the windows in the house and watched the sun set. She shivered as she heard *Minecraft* zombies start moaning from outside. Zombies were easy to beat with a good sword. But that didn't mean they weren't scary!

That reminded her. When it came to beating monsters, it also helped to have good armor. Jaz took her 32 iron ingots out of the furnace. Then she used her crafting table to turn 24 of them into an iron chestplate, leggings, helmet, and boots.

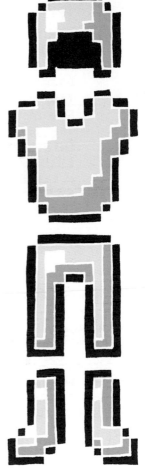

FACT: YOU CAN MAKE *MINECRAFT* ARMOR OUT OF LEATHER, GOLD INGOTS, IRON INGOTS, OR DIAMONDS. IT TAKES EIGHT ITEMS TO MAKE A CHESTPLATE, SEVEN TO MAKE LEGGINGS, FIVE TO MAKE A HELMET, AND FOUR TO MAKE BOOTS.

Jaz had read about knights in shining armor in books. It didn't seem like it would be very comfortable! But the only armor tougher than iron armor in *Minecraft* was diamond armor. It would protect its wearer well.

Still, it was nighttime now. Almost time to go home. Jaz looked out the window again and watched the moon rising. Then she tucked the four pieces of armor into the chest. The next person to visit could wear them.

FACT: THE NIGHTTIME SKY IN *MINECRAFT* HAS STARS AND A MOON. THE MOON HAS PHASES JUST LIKE THE REAL-WORLD MOON. THERE ARE EIGHT STAGES, FROM A FULL MOON TO A NEW MOON.

She also put the sword and the other things in her inventory into the chest. She frowned when she realized she only had one apple and a salmon left. Well, the next visitor could worry about the food supply when they arrived, too.

Would it be Kayla or Dave? Or would Matt come back again? Jaz wasn't sure. But she was happy that she was leaving the place well prepared for the next person. And someday, she decided, she'd be back, too.

Then she stretched out on the orange bed in the little gray house, smiled to herself, and closed her eyes.

The first thing Jaz saw when she opened her eyes again was her sister's face. Kayla was looking down at her. She looked tired. But when she saw that her sister was awake, her expression became very happy.

Jaz sat up. She pulled off the headset and shook her head. Her beaded braids rattled. She glanced at the clock to see what time it was. (It was just before 7 a.m., when they usually got up.) Then she looked back at her sister.

The girls blinked at each other. Then they both smiled. Kayla, who usually wasn't much of a hugger, leaned forward and gave Jaz a big hug.

"You're OK!" she muttered into her twin's shoulder. "I'm so glad. I was worried."

"Why? I'm fine." Jaz decided she wouldn't mention the creeper … or getting lost in the cave. Not yet. Maybe not ever.

"It was so much fun, Kay!" she said instead, folding her legs under herself. "I went exploring and mining and I killed a few spiders and a zombie and I went fishing and built a house … "

"Whoa! Giant *Minecraft* spiders? Sick!" Kayla looked impressed. "Did you get a diamond sword?"

"Not yet." Jaz gave her a long look and a bigger smile. "You need to try it. I bet you could kick zombie butt."

Kayla giggled. "Maybe after Dave visits," she said. "I'll let you guys get it all set up for me before I try."

Jaz didn't press it. She did hug her sister again. Then she got to her feet.

"I'm going to get ready," she said, reaching for the closet door. "I want to get to school early and find Dave and Matt. I just can't wait to tell you three all about it."

Want to Keep Reading?

Turn the page for a sneak peek
at the next book in the series.

MINECRAFT® EXPLORERS

STAYING ALIVE

An Unofficial Minecraft® Adventure

JILL KEPPELER

9781538384091

BEST FRIENDS

. . . .

Friends, Dave Lee mused, were a great thing. Really, they were. But sometimes …

Well, sometimes he wished his friends would be just a little more *careful*.

Take Matt Lopez, for example. Matt was Dave's oldest friend. They'd known each other since they were toddlers.

That's what Dave's mom told him, anyway. He wasn't sure. He just knew he couldn't remember a time they hadn't been friends.

But Matt could be so … so …

"Really, Dave! It's such an adventure! You need to try it."

Yeah, "adventurous" was probably a good word.

ABOUT THE AUTHOR

Jill Keppeler is a writer, editor, reader, geek, gamer, and mom with a background in newspaper journalism. She taught herself to play *Minecraft* when her then-five-year-old son became interested in the game. Now, they play together. Jill lives with her husband and two sons in Buffalo, NY, where she writes, buys too many comic books, cheers for the Sabres and Bills, writes, tries to do lots of cool stuff with her boys, crafts creative cookies, and—oh, yeah—writes.

MINECRAFT® EXPLORERS

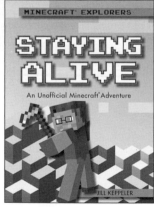
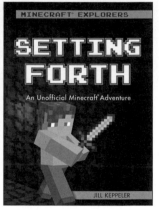

Check out more books at:

www.west44books.com